For baby Teddy Aldrich, with lots of love
~ M C B

For Mormor, Margrethe Kristensen
~ T M

Copyright © 2005 by Good Books, Intercourse, PA 17534
International Standard Book Number: 1-56148-485-7
Library of Congress Catalog Card Number: 2004027641

Text copyright © M. Christina Butler 2005
Illustrations copyright © Tina Macnaughton 2005

Original edition published in English by Little Tiger Press,
an imprint of Magi Publications, London, England, 2005.

Printed in China

Library of Congress Cataloging-in-Publication Data

Butler, M. Christina.
Snow friends / M. Christina Butler ; illustrated by Tina Macnaughton.
p. cm.
Summary: After awakening early from his winter sleep and
wishing for someone to play with, Little Bear is joined by
new friends who help him make a snowman.
ISBN 1-56148-485-7 (hardcover)
[1. Friendship--Fiction. 2. Bears--Fiction.
3. Snowmen--Fiction. 4. Otters--Fiction.
5. Rabbits--Fiction.]   I. Macnaughton,
Tina, ill. II. Title.
PZ7.B98Sn 2005
[E]--dc22

2004027641

Snow Friends

M. Christina Butler
Tina Macnaughton

Good Books

Intercourse, PA 17534
800/762-7171
www.goodbks.com

Little Bear woke early from his deep winter sleep.
As he yawned and stretched, he looked out of the
bear cave and gasped. The world was covered with
a thick white blanket, sparkling in the sunshine!
"Oooh!" he cried, "snow!" and he raced out to play.

Little Bear went rolling and
skidding down the hillside,
racing faster and faster.

He rushed through the trees, shaking the branches to make tiny white snow storms. He stomped and stamped in the crunchy snow, making trails of footprints that circled and twirled.

Little Bear climbed up a hill and gazed out at the whiteness. The mountains and forests were still and silent. He looked around for someone to play with, but he couldn't see anyone . . . anywhere.

"Hellooo!" he cried. "Hellooo!" came back his echo. But no one else replied. Little Bear was all alone.

"Oh dear," he sighed. "If only
I had someone to play with."
And he fell with a plop into
a big snowdrift.

But then Little Bear had an idea. He began
to make a snowball, bigger and bigger.
"If I make a *really* big snowball," he thought,
"I could build a snowman, and *then* I would
have someone to play with!"
So he rolled and rolled a shiny round
snowman body until it was nearly as big
as he was!

Little Bear was so busy with his snowball that he didn't see Otter swimming across the lake.

"Hello!" cried Otter, racing up. "What are you doing?"

"I'm making a snowman. The best snowman EVER!" replied Little Bear.

"Wow!" said Otter. "That sounds like fun. Can I help?"

"That would be great," said Little Bear.
So they pushed and they puffed
until they couldn't roll the snowball
any farther.

Little Bear and Otter stopped for a rest, but just then they heard a muffled voice.

"Hey! What's going on?" it cried. "Everything's gotten dark!"

"My snowball's talking!" squeaked Little Bear.

"No," laughed Otter. "The noise is underneath. Quick!" And together they pushed as hard as they could until the big snowball creaked away to one side.

A rabbit popped up from his burrow.
"Who turned off the light?" he said crossly.

"Sorry," said Little Bear. "We're building the best snowman EVER!"

"And it got stuck on top of your burrow," giggled Otter.

"Funny snowman," said Rabbit, laughing. "It doesn't have a head!"

"We haven't made his head yet," said Little Bear. "You can help if you like."

So Rabbit helped to make
the snowman's head and
gave him a big happy smile.

Then Otter went
back to the river for some
sticks. Little Bear found a few nuts
left in his winter store. Rabbit picked
out the very best
carrot from his
pantry.

They built the snowman together, with Otter's sticks for arms, and the nuts from Little Bear's store for his eyes. Finally Rabbit climbed on to Little Bear's shoulders and pushed the carrot nose in place.

Otter laughed and cheered, "Hurray!"

The BEST SNOWMAN EVER was finished!

For the rest of the day they played
with the snowman in the snow.
They played hide and seek and chase,
and huge snowball fights left them
giggling and gasping for breath.

At last, as the sky turned orange and the sun set, the three friends talked about what games they would play the next day.

"Let's go exploring," said Rabbit.

"But what about Snowman?" said Little Bear. "We can't leave him all on his own."

"Let's build him a friend, then!" said Otter.

So they rolled and patted and shaped
some more, until they made a perfect
little snowman.

By the time they had finished, the stars were
twinkling in the sky. Tired and happy, they crashed
in a heap and watched with wonder as the snowman
and his friend turned to silver in the moonlight.

"He's the BEST SNOWMAN IN THE WORLD,"
whispered Little Bear.

"And he'll never be lonely now that he has a friend,"
said Otter.

"Yes," Rabbit smiled. "Just like us!"